Death & Taxes
5 short stories

PETER CROSS

Copyright © 2024 Peter Cross

All rights reserved.

ISBN: 9798300510169

CONTENTS

Death & Taxes	1
Let There Be Light	18
Twins	26
Better Judgement	36
Election 2024	44

DEATH & TAXES

I apologise to those I will not have the chance to bid farewell to, this sudden departure is not my choice. I am not an evil man but there are those who will seek to portray me in a different, unflattering light. They are distorting the truth, but in these complicated times the truth is not always easy to divine. I will not stay to hear my legacy traduced, to see those close to me hurt by lies. I am undertaking this journey, safe in the knowledge that I will, one day, see those I love in another, better place.

J D W

He re-read the note carefully and signed it above his initials. Straightening slowly he stared blindly at the words, hands in his pockets, head forward. A heavy sigh freed him and he dragged the stool into position below the rope.

***

Gabby stood quietly, intimidated, gazing around the vast open space. To call it a room was an injustice, it was circular, actually a hemisphere, walls curving away on both sides to fade into distant haze. Above her the nacreous roof radiating light and a mysterious warmth, arched upwards into diaphanous cloud. Everything but the faces, hair and hands of her colleagues were drawn in shades of white; the walls that became ceiling and sky, the thousands of loungers strewn as far as she could see, the clothes everyone wore, shimmering opalescent. She ran her hand down her gown and could barely feel the gossamer material. Virginal white, the thought made her smile.

She looked around to observe her countless fellow workers, scattered, receding as far as she could see. Talking, quietly, sitting and standing around, resting between assignments. Placing her tablet on the arm of the nearest lounger she sat to stretch and take it all in. She flicked her gown across her shins, bare feet crossed.

"Hello."

Gabby looked up to see one of her co-workers who had emerged through the wall behind her. "Hello. I'm Gabby."

"Raquel." She stepped closer and Gabby took her offered hand.

Raquel was dressed identically, her white gown confusing the light so that you could never quite focus on it.

"Can I?" She indicated the next lounger and when Gabby nodded, pulled it alongside and perched, smiling.

"You're one of the new cohort, aren't you? Just started?"

Gabby nodded, "Third day."

"How are you getting on?"

"Good so far. Nothing too difficult. They probably give us newbies the easy ones."

"I'm pretty sure it's random, you get what you get." Raquel replied, checking her tablet as she spoke, then setting it aside.

"How long have you been here?" Gabby asked.

Raquel laughed, "Feels like forever, but certainly centuries."

"But you're still here, you must enjoy it."

Raquel frowned slightly, "I suppose, although enjoy is not really the right word. It's rewarding in that you help the clients, well most of them. Of course, there's the odd one that makes you wonder why you do it, but keeps you young as we all say."

Gabby laughed without conviction, it was already the fifth or sixth time she had heard the same joke.

"Yes, I know." Raquel said rolling her eyes, "That and the perfect complexion. Why would anyone give this up?" She held out her hands, palm down and examined her unblemished, dark, radiant skin.

They looked around at their fellow workers. Most were dressed identically, presenting as attractive young men and women, but there were occasional flashes of colour, one or two more flamboyantly dressed.

"Oh, look over there." Gabby pointed, "That's that famous actor. What's his name? I didn't know he'd transitioned?"

"Oh, I know, that was sad, he was so handsome. Car accident, I think. Oh my god, look at him." Raquel was open mouthed and a mischievous look settled. "Want to try something?"

"What do you mean?" Gabby asked, wary at the slight lowering of her companion's voice.

"Of course, you're new, you've probably only channelled for a client."

Gabby frowned, looking across at the actor some distance away. He was dressed in chinos and a shirt, chatting with a woman now clothed in a royal blue ball gown. They were too far away to hear what was being said but he appeared to be asking her to dance.

"What's going on?" Gabby asked. She turned back to Raquel and shrieked in fright her hands flying to her face. The same actor was sat where Raquel had been a moment earlier.

"Oh for fuck's sake, Raquel. You nearly scared me to death."

Raquel's dark brown eyes were now amber and set in the most handsome face Gabby had ever seen. "Oh." Was all she managed as their eyes met.

"How nice to meet you, call me George." Even his voice was suntanned.

Gabby, dumbstruck and starstruck took the actors outstretched hand feeling the strong, warm grip her pale skin almost translucent against his.

"You are so beautiful." he said, "You look like an angel, I have the overwhelming urge to kiss you." The gentle, deep voice carried his smile inside her head.

"Oh I don't think that's allowed." Gabby said, but made no move to withdraw her hand."

"You do know you can choose to channel anyone, don't you, Gabby?" It was his voice and eyes and smile, but Gabby knew she was hearing Raquel.

She paused, thinking, "What anyone?"

"As long as they have transitioned, of course." George replied. "Surprise me."

Gabby thought for a moment and made a decision.

"Excellent choice." George said, with a laugh, easing slightly away and opening his arms in welcome. "I always wanted to meet Liz Taylor."

Gabby glanced down to see her gown replaced with red silk, barely covering the most fabulous breasts. "Oh my god!" She placed her hands over both breasts and squeezed them and laughed, "Look at those babies."

George was doing exactly that and after a moment he stood and extended his hand and she took it and stood too. He was almost a head taller than her and he pulled her gently towards him, his intention quite clear, eyes fixed on her lips.

"Are we allowed to do this?" Gabby asked, resisting gently.

He was nodding, "We are, and actually management encourage it; builds empathy, they say, reminds us of what our clients experience and allows us to understand some of their more irrational life choices."

"If you say so." Gabby turned her face upwards and leant against him.

They kissed for about thirty seconds, or possibly minutes, it was hard to tell. Gabby broke away, breathless.

"Oh my god, wow!" She said, opening her eyes. "Are you feeling that? I thought we'd transcended all that physical …"

George was laughing softly, "Oh yes. Wow indeed."

Ping!

Gabby glanced down at her tablet. The oblong of veined, white marble had become a screen again, now displaying a name, three photographs and below them a list of transactions.

"Ah, back to work." Gabby reluctantly picked up the tablet allowing her appearance to return to her resting state. The vivid, figure hugging dress was replaced by the formless, flowing gown, now draped over a far less voluptuous frame. In her peripheral vision George become Raquel once again.

Ping!

Raquel retrieved the tablet to review her next assignment.

Gabby was frowning at the data on the screen scrolling through the transaction list. She had so far not seen any clients with other than a few minor transactions that needed either repaying or rewarding; this one contained dozens. One after another, every one a credit that need to be repaid.

"Oh sweet." Raquel held her tablet up to show Gabby the usual three images; in this case a young girl, her as a woman and finally as an old lady. "Heart attack." Raquel said. "But 93, so …." She looked down and scrolled the short list of debits. "What a lovely lady, oh, this will be nice." She looked up, "Yours?" and saw Gabby's face. "What?"

Gabby offered her the tablet, looking panicked. Across the top were three chronological images; a young boy, an ordinary looking young man and the last, a hard-faced middle aged man, barely recognisable from his younger self.

Raquel scrolled the list. "Oh fuck! Babe." She looked up at

Gabby, shocked and back down to the list. "This guy's a monster."

"I thought someone like him would be dealt with by someone like you with more experience. I've only just started" Gabby glanced around the room as if searching for help.

"I'm pretty sure it's random, honey. It's just bad luck. I mean, really bad luck, most of us will go through our whole career and never see one like this. What a shitbag, look at what he's stolen, all the credits he's amassed."

Gabby reluctantly took the tablet back. "I'll never get through all of them before he transitions. He's going to take most of it with him." Anger slowly leached into her voice as she scrolled.

"Well, maybe, but look at the top right of the screen. He's a swinger, rope-a-dope; the dumb fuck." Raquel replied, a malicious edge to her voice.

Gabby looked confused and took a moment to understand.

"It means you've got plenty of time." Raquel said quietly, "I reckon you'll get most of them back. Stupid fucker, someone like that really should not hang themselves."

"Oh no!" Gabby gave a little sob and held one hand to her chest. "The first one is just a girl." There were tears in her eyes and she looked pleadingly at Raquel.

Raquel reached over and tapped the task's parameters icon. "Look; that means you don't have to follow the chronological sequence. I've only see this a couple of times before, but where the list of credits is over a certain size you can choose what order you do them in. I think it's so you can deal with the worst ones, the biggest transactions first, sort of even the balance. But honestly, honey, if he was a shooter that might be a consideration, but this sorry excuse for a human has fucked himself. I think you'll get through all of them with time to spare. This scumbag is going to have to face every single one of them by the end."

"What do I do? How do I choose?" Gabby wailed softly, scrolling the list. "Look, 63 of them."

"I'm going to have to go." Raquel waved her tablet, "I've not got the luxury of time for my old lady, but I'd do the ones with the largest transaction values first, the people he's taken the most from. And honestly, any that you want to choose. Also, check that the victims have not already transitioned. If they are still alive they get back what he took. It's not like it never happened to them, but it can make a real difference." She kissed Gabby on the cheek and hugged her. "Also, do them one at a time, come back here each time just to give you time to choose, don't rush it. From his perspective it will be worse too, so, that's what I'd do. Fucker! I've got to go."

Raquel turned and walked towards the wall selecting her first transaction. The doorway materialised and she pressed the bell. Silence, she paused before pushing the door open and stepping into the darkness beyond.

Gabby's heart was beating too fast and she had to calm herself, breathing deeply. This was going to be unpleasant, of that there was no doubt, but she recalled her tutors and her more experienced colleagues saying how satisfying it could be to redress a balance, however little and late. She scrolled slowly down the list and came across a young black woman, strikingly beautiful with the most exquisite bone structure. She was still alive, a teacher now, with a child of her own. But the man had taken almost half of her. How on earth had she survived. Gabby shook her head in wonder at the strength some people possessed. So this beautiful woman, Gloria, would be first. Gabby walked towards the wall with a real sense of purpose, holding down the anger but allowing it to inhabit her. The door appeared and she pressed the button. Sometimes they answered, but there was no sound so she pushed the door and walked through into his mind.

***

'Ding Dong'

What was that? There was no bell on his door. His eyes were closed and the stool had only just passed the point of no return beneath his feet when the image of the tall black woman came to him. She was holding a tablet of some kind.

"Who are you?" How did you get in here?" She seemed so real and was looking at him, stirring a memory, long buried. He wanted to open his eyes to banish the vision, but he could not. She was inside his head and a bolt of fear flashed across his mind.

An image appeared to him projected in space and he knew she could see it too. It was as if they were watching a film together, this tall attractive stranger, trespassing in his consciousness. He was drawn with a seeping dread to the suspended scene. That room; his pulse jumped and a tiny noise escaped him.

"You pathetic, stupid, idiot." she said, her voice heavy with a contempt so thick he could taste it. "Hanging yourself. Seriously. It's going to take you a lifetime to die, and I'm going to be here to ensure your debts are all repaid."

"I beg your pardon." He was outraged. "Do not talk to me like that young lady." He stared at her, the blue dress, her cleavage her long elegant legs. "Do I know you?"

"Sadly, yes. Let me remind you."

She tapped the tablet and the scene began to play in this most claustrophobic, intimate cinema.

"Turn that off." His inner voice had a frightened edge.

She ignored him and now the moving image floated in front of them. There she was, in the film, this same woman in the blue dress walking into an office. A large desk and a long couch and armchair and a man sat at the desk with an old fashioned phone to his ear.

"What the …" the man said quietly. "That's me, that's …"

In the scene, the woman walked across the room and the man stood and indicated the sofa.

They shook hands

"Sit there, make yourself comfortable." He appraised her, openly staring carefully at her breasts and then sliding a hand down from her waist over her curved hip as one might a thoroughbred horse.

The woman froze, her alarm and discomfort filled the room but failed to touch the man.

"Drink?" he asked, walking across to the cabinet at the far wall where he poured himself a shot of Bourbon. He turned to see her shaking her head.

"I guess you've not done this before." he said. "You must

have had other auditions."

"Well yes, but ..." Her nerves and fear stifled her response, her hands, jittery, moving without purpose.

"Why don't you let me get a better look at you, Gloria, take of the dress, but keep your heels on.

"What, take off ..."

"Yes honey, lose the dress, I need to see what we're investing in."

"But I don't ..."

"Do you want he job or don't you? You decide, If you do, take off the dress, if you don't, then get out, go back to being a waitress or whatever you do. But don't take too long." He took a mouthful of bourbon and waited.

The image froze, hanging in space, marking the precise moment in time after which her life would never be the same. Gabby willed her to say no, to walk, already knowing what had happened all those years ago. In the near darkness of his mind, there was just the sound of his heavy breathing.

"Remember me now?" Gloria asked, quietly.

In the reflected light of the image she could see him looking at her. Even now he could not prevent himself looking at her breasts.

"I don't understand, what do you want, where did you get this film?" He was not so sure of himself now; metaphorically and physically off balance.

"It's your memory of what you did to me. Do I need to play it forward, do you need to see me remove the dress and then for you to put your fingers inside me and then to rape me. Shall we play that through?"

His mouth was working but no sound came out.

"We could do, Gloria continued. I've played it over in my mind a million times and I can tell you the shame, self-loathing and disgust never fade. I tried to kill myself and failed. But a decent man saved me and then I saved myself, so that you don't get to win."

"Honey, that's just the way it was back then, that's how it worked." Pleading soaked his words.

"Oh you piece of shit. Really!"

"The world's not always a nice place, I wasn't the only one."

"Ok, you lump of human excrement, it's time to repay the debt. That's my memory in your head, a piece of my soul and I'm taking it back. When I do you'll understand that memory is not a discrete thing, not an object. Your memory of me is tied to lots of your other memories. I don't need them or want them, but they will be taken too. Think of it as tax for holding a piece of me all this time."

"What the fuck are you talking about you stupid bitch. Fuck off!"

She smiled at him without as trace of kindness on her face and reached up to hold the top of the floating image. Now it was more than light, it had physical form and rippled like silk in her grasp. She felt the alarm flood into him. In the 'real', world, the rope tightened around his neck, gravity drawing him in. His eyes were suddenly wide, fear writ large, his mouth open.

As she slowly began to pull the image, tearing the light, he howled. "No, No, No!"

She continued to rip the memory from him and his screams filled the room well after the light folded into her hand and disappeared. She waited until there was only darkness and the soundtrack of his whimpering and let herself out.

***

The light in the auditorium was blinding after the darkness and Gabby took a moment, her back against the door, eyes closed. She opened her eyes when she felt Raquel's hand on her arm, to see her concerned look.

"I'm fine. Honestly."

"Was it bad?" Raquel asked.

"Not as bad as I thought. He's unrepentant. Unbelievable. But, actually, that makes it so much easier." She looked down.

"No, don't." Raquel said.

"What?" Gabby looked up.

"Don't waste your pity on him."

"I'm not. I was feeling a little guilty, actually. I enjoyed taking those memories back, retrieving a piece of her soul, repaying the debt. Or at least not allowing him to own it."

"Good. Come on, who's next. How long did that take?"

Gabby checked the tablet and laughed, "five milliseconds of his time. You're right I can get them all."

Raquel was nodding, "It's unbelievable, isn't it. He's an American for God's sake, doesn't he own a gun. You'd have been lucky to repay more than a couple if he'd blown his brains out. When they hang themselves it takes about four minutes of their time to die and that's hours and hours for us."

Gabby took a deep breath and checked the screen. Gloria's account had been repaid in full and somewhere in the world that brave woman would sense the change, she might not know why, but something tiny would shift. Then, maybe in a day or so, in their time, she might hear the news and maybe realise what it was.

Gabby showed Raquel another profile for one of the transactions. "So, this woman caught my eye. Look what he took from her. Tiny slivers of her soul, slice by slice."

"Have you viewed the memory?" Raquel asked.

"No, but look at the time scale, it went on for years. That's a lot of memories, it's going to hurt like fuck when I take all of that back, isn't it."

Raquel was nodding again, "Oh yes that's going to tear a hole in his mind."

'Ding Dong'

Again, no sound. Gabby became Mary and stepped through the door into the darkness in which she had left him. She commanded his eyes open and they looked together, at the room, barely altered in the sliver of time that had passed since they last looked. The stool had tipped a fraction further, close to toppling, the rope a little tighter. She closed his eyes and presented her image and heard his intake of breath.

"Mary."

"Yes Jimmy, it's me."

A noise, somewhere between a whimper and a groan escaped him. "We don't need to do this, Mary. I'm sorry."

"Oh Jimmy, we do."

His inner eye could not be closed and the scene played out in his mind for them both to watch. Mary was a rather plain, slim woman, not really his type, but she was unbelievably efficient as his personal assistant and needed the job badly. He paid her more than he needed to in order to ensure that she would not leave.

The scene played and Mary entered the same office with a coffee cup on a small tray. She was dressed in a modest skirt and blouse.

"Please, Mary, we don't need to do this." He was pleading.

"How many times, Jimmy, how many times? Every week or so for what, six years."

"Why didn't you leave if you hated it so much. I think you secretly loved it." His anger and defiance were rising again; after all this was just Mary who had always done his bidding.

In the replayed image she walked across to the desk and placed the tray on the corner.

"Let's have a bit of fun." The young Jimmy said, sitting forward in his chair.

The image froze and Gabby, as Mary, spoke to him, "Lets have a bit of fun. That's what you always said." Loathing carried the words through his mind. She shook her head and the film began again, his inner eye unable to unsee the images. She played five memories, all basically the same, the disgusting, wet sounds and then his feral grunts and her choking.

Then she summoned every scene from his mind which held a part of Mary and the countless images rose together and hung in the air like layers of fine silk. She turned to watch him as she grasped the top edge and slowly began to tear them all away.

His screams should have been appalling, might have induced pity in a fellow human. His mind was bleeding and she was happy that these would be some of his final moments.

Darkness descended again. She opened the door and turned, framed by light. "Lots more, Jimmy, I'll be back before you know it."

***

Gabby took a moment to compose herself again, resting against the wall, focussing only on the iridescent light, the warmth on her skin.

Raquel was waiting and smiled. "Ok, looks like you have this."

"Yes." Gabby was breathing intentionally. "I guess his pain is only in proportion to the evil he brought."

"That's the whole point, everyone gets what they deserve in the end. For some, people like him, vengeance is mine ... and all that" Raquel spoke quietly a hand on Gabby arm.

"Yes." Gabby smiled at her and then stepped back and slowly spread her beautiful wings wide and high and with a swift, smooth downward movement lifted herself momentarily off the floor. She folded them away as she looked back at her tablet to scroll the list of his other victims.

"Time to pay." She turned and pressed the bell.

'Ding Dong'

This time there was a scream from behind the door. She smiled, grimly at Raquel before she opened it and stepped into the darkness of his bleeding mind.

******

LET THERE BE LIGHT

Free at last. Well, that only took 100,000 years! I should be clear, that's your years, it's hard to say how long it took from my perspective. Also, if I'm being honest, it might actually be anything from 5,000 years to a million and billions of generations of my kind, of which I am the final one. As I said, it's hard to translate into your time frame; relativity and all that. 'Let there be light', It's a snappy line but in practice it's no small task building a star and making it shine.

Anyway, that's history now and I'm on my way, along with a shockingly large number of my brethren. I had no say in which direction I left the yellow dwarf star which you, parochially, call your sun, but as it happens I'm heading your way along with a load of my mates. Most of us get fired off across space, gradually moving away and apart from the legion of fellow photons that departed together, spreading out forever. The only thing that's certain, so they tell us, is that in space we're all travelling at the same speed, a number 'they' decided to call 'c' (for the Latin scholars out there, apparently from celeritas) – don't ask me!

If I'm honest, it's a lonely business and I'm rather looking forward to landing on that gorgeous looking planet up ahead and doing my bit to keep it warm and flourishing. Simple enough maths, 8 of your minutes, that's how long it's going to take to get to you. Sadly, when I arrive it's a complete lottery as to where I end up. But from out here it does look inviting;

everywhere else I look it's just dark. There's so little of anything out here, mostly nothing, actually. Well, once again I'm simplifying. As soon as you look closely, there's quite a lot of stuff, it's just rather spread out. Not so much where I am now, just on the outskirts of a star; quite busy here. As I whizz away there are lumps of 'stuff' flying past all the time. They might be scarce, but with so many of us leaving the sun all the time, these tiny lumps (you call them atoms) are constantly getting whacked. Not that they're bothered either way, they just absorb us and immediately fire out one of us in a random direction. But oddly each offspring photon is imbued with a little of the atomy personality from where they emerged. If you managed to catch some of those next generation photons you could tell what type of atom they got born in; which is neat.

I digress. Space is pretty empty from your perspective, and actually from mine too, so it's nice to have a proper destination and there's every chance that I'll make it, at least as far as the atom soup that's settled around your lump of fertile rock. So for now, I'm just going to zip along, at my top speed of 'c' and I'll get back to you in about seven minutes when I arrive in your neck of the solar system.

***

You are so lucky, Wow! As I got closer it was quite trippy, if I'm honest. Almost nothing anywhere —the odd far off star firing the occasional photon back at me, and here you seem to have life. Crazy. I'm not sure how this works, but look at all this organisation out of nothing, it's a bloody mystery, I mean what are the odds?

Anyway, your blue, green marble is approaching fast, filling my field of view, as it were, and that means there's now quite a lot of atomy 'stuff' out here, at least by space standards. A few of my fellow travellers are starting to smack into what I understand you call your atmosphere. I keep glimpsing weird looking lumps of stuff; bigger than those tiny ones I passed on the way over. Looks like we're going to lose about a quarter of us on the way through this soup and the rest of us are going to end up on the surface, or should I say, in the surface.

Bam! I don't know exactly what I hit, but whatever it was, it's the end of my journey, but not this story, because I'm handing the narrative on to my successor.

***

So, the massive lump of stuff my predecessor just smacked into after their 93 million mile journey, turns out to be a molecule you call cadmium red. The cadmium bit is one of those lumpy atom things we talked about earlier. Same idea as the simple ones we passed in space, but much more complicated and much bigger. The intelligent (really?) systems on this planet seem to be able to create layers of these atoms all held together so that there's no way for us get past them. My predecessor and gazillions of his cohort smacked into one of these layers and that's them done. But as Pops (anthropomorphize, Moi!) mentioned, not the end of the story, because I got created in the lump of cadmium. In your terms, I'm not quite my father's son because the thing you call frequency (colour is easier) got changed. Pops would have self-identified as blue, whereas I'm most definitely red. Also I got shot out of the Cadmium atom in a completely different direction to the one pops arrived in, headed, by chance, for a very special location and fate.

I mentioned organised systems, aka life, on this already improbable affront to entropy, well I'm headed for one of them and for one very particular part of this 'life'. Now these 'lifes' are enormous; not sun or planet enormous, but bloody massive from my perspective. You need about, (and I'm going to set this out longhand, for effect) 7,000,000,000,000,000,000,000,000,000 of these lumpy atom things and a whole variety of them too, (there are well over a hundred different types), to make one 'person'. I've no idea what that is, obviously, but that's what this type of life is called here. And, as if that number wasn't vast, you can't just jumble all these atoms in a pile; the way you connect them up is important. Imagine how may ways there are of organising that number of things. I'd say it's implausible that you end up with anything useful, let alone something so functional as a 'person'; but I'm just passing this on, so don't shoot the messenger.

Anyway, a fraction of a second after I got ejected from that cadmium atom I smacked into one of these 'person' things. In I went passing most of the way through an 'eye' where I got absorbed by a really fancy set of atoms that they call 'retinal'. So, not much of a life story for me then; fired out of a cadmium atom, dodged a few stray soup atoms over a few meters and wham, goodnight photon. It's the end of the line for me and at this point things get really weird, so I'm going to have to pass you over to our narrator, who cannot be seen but pervades everything; look don't blame me, this is the shit they feed me I'm just passing it on. Take it or leave it.

***

LET THERE BE LIGHT

Hi there. The 'red' photon asked me to talk you through what happens next. Without wanting to minimise their contribution, had they been the only photon in the vicinity not a lot would have happened at this point. Their parent, Pops, the dude who made the journey all the way from the edge of the sun's photosphere 93 million miles away, ended up absorbed by a cadmium atom in a layer of pigment. But Pops was far from alone, they were accompanied by sextillions of others like them, all leaving the sun in the same second (and if you were wondering, a sextillion is a lot!) A bunch of those fellow travellers suffered the same fate as Pops, absorbed into cadmium atoms and each atom then fired out an offspring photon. Being 'born' in cadmium, each of these next geners had a characteristic red colour and they whizzed off, randomly, in all directions, in their sextillions. As it happens, quite a few hit the same small part of the 'person' that happened to be close by on the earth's surface at that moment.

Because one of these truly fancy creations intercepted a slug of these photons something weird happened next. If she (yes, she, don't ask, it's complicated) had not been there, the stream of red photons would likely have whacked into some other inanimate object and might well have been absorbed and re-emitted again in a sort of pinball cascade. At some point there would be too little energy left for their children or grandchildren to spawn another offspring and then the journey would truly be over. Each smudge of energy that started in the centre of the sun thousands of years ago would have travelled across space and been smeared across many atoms on planet Earth and would ultimately have ended up as heat, a sort of poor person's light, that makes atoms wobble a bit more than they would otherwise do.

But, that's not what happened to our little band of photons, oh no, the avalanche they started is so much more interesting. They ended up in a very sophisticated 'detector'. Somehow, these organic people machines (and lots of other types of organic machines on the planet) have managed to acquire what they call chromophores, a fancy name for a collection of atoms that can grab a photon and not let it go. You really couldn't make this up, but the arrival of the photon causes some fancy circuitry to send a message through some more fancy circuitry up a sort of chain of command. The message being 'red photon arrived'. Now, as I said earlier, if you had just one of these photons arriving, it's a non-event. Imagine trying to start your own Mexican wave in a football stadium; forget it. However, if a 1,000 of you all wave at the same time then you're probably going to get some traction.

From this point on it's more or less magic I'm afraid, so take it or leave it. A 'signal' goes up the line and the most complicated piece of machinery in the known universe 'decides' what to do about this. Some fancy circuitry automatically checks to see if this 'Red stuff' has happened before, the circuits (their owners call them neurons and synapses) attempt to match the nearest similar thing to see if there are already patterns in other circuits similar to the 'incoming reds' event. This matching thing is not a one-off, the circuits are getting messages constantly and are at this 24/7 looking for anything matching a pattern already in the system. More of the reds arrive and the pattern shifts a bit as the circuits keep on their constant search. Also, don't get too hung up on the 'reds' bit of the message. If the vast array of circuits find a similar pattern but it happens to be blue or green, it might be a close enough match for them to get agitated and for the magic to continue. In this case messages gets sent to other parts of the machine as it tries to work out what might happen next. This is actually the really clever bit, it's not just magic it's future fiction magic. The machine makes a 'guess' at what's about to happen while all the time watching the incoming messages from the various pattern matching circuits to decides if this prediction is interesting enough to go up the chain of command. This particular one makes it all the way to the top table, to the head of operations so that resources can be allocated to deal with the 'red'. All the while, of course, photons of many colours are arriving by the bucket load from all directions and are being checked for possible matches against previous configurations experienced and stored. And all of this in, literally. The blink of an eye; like I said, you couldn't make this stuff up.

You've probably lost the plot at this point, so here's the summary, in terms that one of these human machines would understand: A human was about to cross a road when in her peripheral vision she 'saw' a red sports car approaching. She stopped and waited and watched it pass and then crossed. The only way she knew that the massive conglomeration of atoms was approaching and avoided a collision was thanks to our travelling photon and their myriad companions raining down from the sun. Wild!

******

LET THERE BE LIGHT

TWINS

"Stand Clear of the doors!"

It was obvious to the people standing in the open entrance of the carriage that the two of them would try to beat the trap. They were sprinting, her leading, hair flying. She squealed as she leapt between the closing doors despite knowing that he could not possibly make it. She cannoned into the tall businessman who twisted to avoid a direct collision and the heel of her shoe broke as she stumbled into him.

"For gods sake!"

It was halfway to a shout, but loud in the confined tube train and his irritation was mirrored across the wall of faces that recoiled from her reckless energy. He was holding her denim jacket, fending her off, preventing her from falling.

The boy managed an arm between the closing jaws and his body crashed into the face of the door. He had done enough of course and the guard, shouting, "Stand Clear!" was forced to cycle the doors and he jumped in.

"Sorry. Thanks." The girl glanced up at the businessman who released her jacket and returned to his phone with a frown and a theatrical shake of his head. All the other phones were being raised too, the micro-drama over.

"Oh shit, look." The girl pulled her shoe off and showed the boy the dangling heel.

"It'll glue." He was panting, "Just don't lose it."

She kissed him on the mouth and everyone carefully

ignored them, fitting into their new positions, maximising the distance to their nearest neighbour as the tube jerked and accelerated out of the station. The commuter rush hours were almost over but Kings Cross is busy on weekday evenings and the carriage was full. Not, bodies pressed together full, but more intimate than most wanted. Most. There are some happy to be forced against a fellow traveller of their desired sex.

Ahmed, shorn of the momentary reckless air, became the young man that he was. He glanced around the carriage assessing his fellow travellers. Reading the poster about unwanted contact from strangers, assault, and the need to call it out, he wondered what he would do if someone did that to his girlfriend. His gaze traced her profile. He was hopelessly entranced by her and her worldliness, her shocking and completely thrilling attitude to sex. He blushed at the new memories of her guiding him and encouraging him and had to look away to quell the instant arousal.

Jody, the leaping girl had quietly transformed too and as a composed, self-assured young woman was calmly gazing around the carriage. She caught Ahmed looking at her and knew what he was thinking about. He was sweet. Ridiculously naïve, particularly about sex, but so many other things too. In retrospect it was amazing that he had ever asked her out. Serendipity in seeing him twice in two days at the coffee shop, his handsome face and surprisingly polite manner; it was just how the world worked, sometimes. She was not inclined to overthink it. Of course, she had had to prompt him, heavily, to illicit that first invitation. She had never dated a Muslim boy and it was interesting, a first for her. Growing up in North London, she lived in an ethnic world as diverse as one could find anywhere. People used the words 'black' and 'white', but as far as she could tell, everyone was, more or less, brown, all a little the same, and a little not. But still, most people stayed within their tracks; she had no Muslim friends and few 'white' ones. They were the same age, both having finished university, both with good degrees and both struggling to find a job. But summer was not yet over and everyone was telling her to chill out, everything would be fine, she would be working for the rest of her life.

The train suddenly slowed and caught her off balance; she bumped into the business man again, "Sorry."

He ignored her.

The crowded carriage thinned as they headed south; many left to shop on Oxford street and more at Victoria and Vauxhall. Now there were a few empty seats and she quickly moved to one and pulled Ahmed beside her.

A moment later she saw him. Well, she had seem him earlier, the boy with the large rucksack, but he had been facing away from her, now she watched him scan along the carriage. Too quick, too nervous, but that was not it. Her mind took seconds to join the dots and it was so unlikely that she rejected the idea. She turned away from the boy toward Ahmed beside her and he glanced up from his phone. This just could not be happening and she was still constructing the logic, the host of things that would have to be true for this to be real.

Whatever Ahmed caught on her face alarmed him. "What?" He glanced at the man in the seat beside her, but he was engrossed, watching his phone, earPod deaf. "What?" Ahmed looked around the other passengers and she watched his eyes glide past the young man and slam back.

His mouth fell open. "Shit."

It was barely a whisper and could not have frightened her more.

"Is it him?" she asked, unwilling to turn to look.

Her words were too low to hear against the sound of the doors closing but he heard them anyway.

She watched his jaw clench and the colour drain from his face as he too time travelled towards an appalling near future that fit the facts of what he could see. He nodded slowly.

"Oh, Jesus." she whimpered. They had spoken about him briefly just once, the rumours; her imagination ran of control.

Ahmed's eyes were closed and they were holding hands, being shaken as the train barrelled beneath London, heading for Pimlico, a minute away.

He opened his eyes and looked at her and the relief she felt in his calm was overwhelming.

He spoke slowly, "I'm going to talk to him. When the train stops, try to get as many people off as you can without panicking them." He made sure she was taking this in, "Stop the door closing, if you have to, but be quick, try to get everyone out."

She was nodding and her pulse slowed for a moment as she processed his words and then accelerated again. Her heart rattled inside her, synchronised with the train in the tunnel. A tiny noise escaped her and she thought for a moment that she might wet herself, fear dimming her vision. Her world was out of focus, blurred to meaningless noise, her mind, for a moment, unable to construct an acceptable reality. His hand holding hers drew her slowly back as the train began to coast and then brake.

"Wait until he sees me and I start talking to him and then tell people." He was looking at her as she blinked him into focus. "Ok?"

She nodded; he was not even sure she could stand, but there was nothing he could do. He kissed her on the cheek and stood, bracing against the slowing train. Grabbing the overhead bar he took two steps towards the next set of doors and the young man with the large rucksack leaning against the glass partition. Ahmed's movement triggered the man's peripheral vision. He turned and Ahmed watched his eyes widen in shock. Pushing himself away from the glass, he held the handrail as the slowing train threatened to overbalance him and the large pack he was carrying.

"Mo." Ahmed said taking two more steps, close now, "As-salamu alayk."

They were identical twins, separated since Ahmad left for university and Mohammad left home, disappeared, no one knew where; or would not say.

"Three years, brother, where are you going?"

Mohammad was panicking, his free hand making uncontrolled movements his eyes scanning Ahmad frantically, disbelieving that it could be his twin.

Ahmed kept talking, holding his brothers eyes. Those so, so familiar eyes that he saw in the mirror every day, but now filled with fear and confusion.

"Where are you going, little brother; with that big rucksack?"

The familiar jibe jolted Mohammad back, "Three minutes, you old man." Mohammad replied, automatically. The words, their eternal joust, retained their old rhythm, and closed out the thousand days since they had last spoken as if it were yesterday. But it was not yesterday and the young man facing Ahmed was a very different twin.

The train jerked to a stop and as the doors screeched open behind Mohammad, Ahmed sensed Jody behind him her voice low but urgent.

Mohammad was watching her moving quickly from person to person. "What's she doing?" the first trace of alarm.

"She's my girlfriend. She's pretty, isn't she."

Mohammad's mouth dropped open and he stared, disbelieving at Ahmed and then back to the girl, watching her, transfixed.

"She should cover herself. You should make her cover herself." Mohammad's anger rose.

This forced a small laugh from Ahmad, "Mo, bruv she does as she pleases, she's smart –"

"Why are you with a woman like that, bro." Mohammad's brow was creased, concern for his fallen twin, plain to see.

"Because she's smart and pretty and nice, and I like her and she likes me."

Mohammad's condemnation was instant, "She looks like a prostitute."

"She looks like every other woman around here, bruv and the fact that you don't like the way she dresses is your problem not hers."

The riposte was more heavy handed than Ahmed had intended and Mohammad stiffened. "What's happened to you, bro, have you forgotten all your teachings?"

Ahmed held his brother's gaze, aware that the carriage was emptying, movements and sounds too brittle and tight to be normal. On the platform he avoided looking at the people hurrying away, glancing over their shoulders as they fled. Fear, palpable in the frantic movements and hushed voices.

"Mo, Bruv, where do you think I've been for the last three

years. All I've done is learn."

"Learn their lies."

They stared at one another, an island of quiet, each tracking forward from their inseparable childhood, the telepathic intimacy of identical twins, that moment of abrupt severance and loss and now this. People moving away, sounds fading, leaving them stranded, bound together in this unlikely place.

"Lies, why would people teach me lies?" Ahmed said quietly and saw another kind of fear grow in his twin's eyes. "No, bruv, it's still me, still your brother who loves you and will always love you." He lowered his voice now as a the last ambient, human sounds ebbed from the tunnel. "But when you learn things you change. That's the point. I see you have changed too little brother; it's just that we've learned different things."

There was no announcement, the doors suddenly began to close and Mohammad twisted to looked around at the almost empty platform. Ahmed tensed, ready to grab his brother if he tried to leave the carriage, but the limb of the door passed before he could react and they were trapped. The train did not move and Muhammad stared at his brother, a complex flow of emotions crossing his young face.

"What have you done, what's happening."

"Bruv, all I've done is talk to you." Ahmed said, opening his palms in the universal gesture of trust.

Mohammad's eyes danced up and down the empty carriage in disbelief. He twisted to see through the door and watched a tall man in a London Underground uniform leading Jody away. She was looking over her shoulder, limping, fear and tears bright on her cheeks.

"What's in the rucksack, Mo?" Ahmed asked quietly.

Mohammad stared at him, calculating, understanding that whatever he had intended would, now, not happen. His shoulders dropped and his lips began to tremble. He shook his head.

"Mo, bruv. I'm here. We can fix this."

"You've ruined it."

"What, what have I ruined? Where were you going?"

"It doesn't matter now, I've failed. My mission is over."

"Your mission! Bruv what are you talking about? Mo, where were you going?"

Mohammad slid to the floor leaning his pack against the door, his legs straight, head slumped forward.

"Talk to me Mo, what's in the rucksack?"

Mohammad looked up, "You don't understand, bro, they are disrespecting us, killing our people all over the world, we have to show them we are strong, we have to strike back."

"Strike, how? Who are you striking on a Thursday night in South London?" As he said the words, a dreadful possibility dawned. "Oh shit, bruv, not the Academy."

The clenched jaw and defiant look were all the answer he needed.

Ahmed slid to the floor, back against the partition his feet almost touching his brother's. "That's where we were going, Jody and me, to the gig at the Brixton Academy. You were going to try to kill me." He said quietly.

The silence stretched and stretched between them and tears overflowed Mohammad's eyes.

"Not you Bro, all the deviants, all the sodomites, not you."

"Oh Mo." It was almost a sob, a lament for someone who had passed. "You want to kill people who listen to five young women in a rock band."

"Degenerate whores."

"Where is this coming from, Mo, why are you so angry? You never used to be."

"That's because we were brainwashed, they hid the truth from us while they were killing our people all over the world. Afghanistan, Syria, the Holy Land, everywhere." He brushed his tears away, angrily.

Ahmed retreated, replaying the last time they had been together, the day he left for university almost three years earlier. He had not believed Mohammad when he said he was leaving too, to study; bravado, just words. Their parents had not told him when Mohammad disappeared. It was his mother's tears when he returned home at the end of his first term that forced him to believe what they told him. His father had been strangely quiet, but his language suggested he believed both his sons were out in the world 'learning'. Ahmed had wondered whether he knew where Mohammad was, but he had never dared ask his father, directly; now the regret knifed through him, physical pain in his chest.

"Dad knew where you were, didn't he?" He fixed Mohammad, drawing the defiant response.

"Knew! Bro, he sent me, said one of his son's had to defend Islam."

"Sent you; where?"

"Manchester."

"That's where you've been for three years, Manchester?"

"Learning the truth, preparing for this moment, preparing for jihad and to bring honour to our family."

Ahmed's chest was tight. "So you think mum would have been proud to see both her sons dead along with lots of other young people."

Mohammad's head tilted forward.

Ahmed's eyes flooded with tears. "How many of us did you think you would kill?" he asked quietly.

There was no response, no movement, just the sound of the air conditioning fans, suddenly deafening.

"I mean, you're going to have to kill a lot of us, Mo, to bring about your new world where women are treated like possessions and –"

"Shut up!" Mohammad looked up, crying and angry. "What do you know, you have a whore for a girlfriend, I bet you don't even pray now, perhaps you deserve to die."

"What do I know?" Ahmed was nodding slowly. "What do I know? What have I learned? Good question, little brother; what indeed." He blinked away the tears to see his brother's tortured face. "Do you even know what I was studying at university?"

There was no reply, just an implacable stare and the silence between them stretched out.

Finally, Ahmed said, "What I learned is that people are just people and that most of them are kind and that we would be better trying to understand each other than kill each other. Oh, and that Edinburgh is bloody cold in winter. They call it philosophy, the degree I did and that's what I learned."

He could hear subdued movement, stifled sound and glanced along the carriage. Out of sight of Mohammad the connecting door eased very slowly ajar and there was the sound of something metallic rolling along the floor towards them. The door closed again. His twin looked up and they held each other's gaze.

"I'm with you little bro, it's all going to be fine."

******

BETTER JUDGEMENT

God here. Or whatever moniker your lot chooses for me, and if you're not a fan, well that's fine, think of me as whatever fills the unseen places in the universe. Anyway, enough of the metaphysics. I heard some of you debating the whole 'free will' thing and having just watched you make a judgement on a specific borderline case I see many of you have this back to front, or upside down. Let me start by explaining what happened to, let's call him Pete; not his name, but I know how you like names. I'll sketch the final scene for you and the judgement that was handed down and then we can work backwards to where this all started to go pear shaped.

Here's what happened:
Pete is trapped, exposed on the street in the drizzle, cold and wet, the stranger almost within touching distance. Overwhelmed, almost paralysed with fear, he knows he has no choice and pulls the trigger. A dagger flash of light; the kick of the gun; the percussive violence radiating outwards; blood, bone and brain tissue splattered across the wall. A moment ago what was just a thought, is now grimly, entropically manifest. The dying man slumps to the ground, in that slice of time transformed from a father and husband to an unstable, cooling collection of atoms. Pete, terrified, stands dumb in the face of a conspiring universe.

Not a complicated one for your rule makers; he was easy to catch, barely tried to conceal what he had done. The prosecutors had little trouble in making their case and the jury made short work of choosing permanent incarceration. The defence argued that he was damaged, that this was inevitable. They claimed he was not really responsible, but your 'justice' scales tilted to him having pulled the trigger in 'free will'. Certainly, with my 'all seeing omnipresence' I can confirm that however many times you replay that moment Pete will shoot the innocent man. Pete's mind, instantiated in his physical brain, and the author of his corporeal intent, was in a state that meant he exercised no effective 'free will', at least in the broad sense you lot like to think of it: a 'considered' choice made in circumstances where another was available (for example, not pulling the trigger!).

Given your inability to encompass all of time and space, as I do (although in this case we're merely discussing the internal space inside Pete's skull) I'm going to explain what got us, well him, here. So, if you're looking for a more nuanced answer, and you should be, you need to zoom out with me. I'll wind back time for you to see if we can find a moment, if one existed, where these two lives were doomed.

Four hours earlier

Pete had not taken his meds, again. He'd been skipping for a while now, knowing he needed to be ready, sharp otherwise they would almost certainly find him and kill him as they had tried to do before. He feels their closing presence and his quiescent anxiety begins its familiar ascent. It is dusk, only an hour or so until dark when he might escape, might slip down the side alley and disappear into the city where he will be hard to track. Lights out, curtains open, he sits in the chair set back from the window. Hyper-alert, he scans the street and waits, leg bouncing, twitching as he tries to control the fear and rising panic. But he's a sitting duck. Coat on and out the back door he creeps, pulling it carefully, quietly, closed. The steady rain softens the night but concealed in the dark alley away from the street light's steady gaze he is soon drenched. How long until it is safe? The cold and damp seeping into him decide that.

He thinks the coast is clear, the residential street empty, hushed by the relentless drizzle. He slips from shadow, hand on the gun in his pocket, just in case. He has taken only a few steps when the man turns the corner and comes straight for him. He raises the gun in self defence and the man freezes, eyes wide. He looks ordinary, vaguely familiar, but that's how they get you, he is almost certainly a highly trained agent. But Pete has the drop on him, but for how long, how many of them are there? There will be backup. He has no choice.

So, no help there, no free will available to allow Pete and the innocent man an alternative ending. We need to go back further:

A Year Earlier

Pete had promised her it would not happen again, He pleaded, but knew that line of her jaw, that cruel set of her beautiful features. Now he watches from the window as she lifts the suitcase into the taxi and without looking back, climbs in. His tears are hot and silent as the cab blurs and slides away. She is gone, forever, and the void she filled, he knows, will remain empty. He has to start taking his meds again.

Five Years Earlier

He understands the words, but they make no sense. How could smoking a little weed have done this? He knows the doctors are right, but also that they must be wrong, because it is impossible. But, the pills did make it go away, dissolved the fear, allowed him to remember who he is, so even if they are wrong, probably better to take them and 'pretend' their diagnosis is right. He isn't even sure he knows what schizophrenia is, exactly; something crazy people have, certainly not him. Still, if the pills make him feel better, best play along, at least for now.

Fifteen Years Earlier

Oh my god! He is immersed in golden bliss, floating. It is the most beautiful feeling he has ever experienced. He is going to do this again, and again, and again and …

Thirty Years Earlier

It's a boy! A perfect, healthy newborn son, to be loved and cherished and nurtured. Unique. Doomed?

OK, we obviously missed it. There's no way this baby boy is destined to shoot a man in the face in thirty years time in a street which does not even exist yet (we'll get to determinism shortly!).

I need to look a little closer; One second …

Oh yes, there it is, I missed it; such a tiny moment, but now I see it, it's obvious.

Two Weeks Earlier

He stands at the sink staring at the small brown bottle without seeing it, his mind tilted inwards. He knows he's not really sick, knows he'll be fine without them; better even, because, somehow they shrink him and his world. He also knows he should keep on taking them or bad things might happen. Round and round the thoughts go. The bottle is in his hand, but he remembers her, the scent of her, her soft skin under his hands, the profound pleasure in holding her close. He focusses again on the bottle and knows that without the pills he might never share that with someone again. But he is certain he is not really ill and desperately needs to feel like himself again, to remember who he is. He places the bottle back in the cupboard and closes the mirrored door and tries not to drown in his own tortured gaze.

That was it, that point, that tiny span of time where Pete exercised his free will. In those moments he could have made a different choice, because if we replay those frames 1,000 times he will make that other choice, to start taking his pills again, 73 times. OK, hold it down, I hear the complaining loud and clear, 'his brain in that state could only have produced one outcome'. As a deity, time is more flexible for me than it is for you physically constrained entities, so I actually did replay the moment 1000 times and so I know this to be the case.

OK, calm down, Please! I can hear you without the shouting. Look, I know determinism seems appealing to your arrogant little minds, but, without wanting to be rude, you know so little about how the universe really works. I realise you can often 'completely' predict what something will look like or be like or do in a few seconds. It works pretty well for 'big' things, cars, snooker balls, ballistic missiles (you stupid ****ers). But, as you already know you can't actually do this when things get tiny, when the illusion of what you, simplistically, call particles evaporates and the true smeary nature of things emerges. I know some of you believe you just need to measure stuff better, but that delusional galleon sailed into the sunset decades ago. No, there's a scale at which, 'shit happens', as you might like to phrase it. Those of you who think I'm a managing director, universe CEO style thing and assume I can fix stuff, sorry to disappoint you, but that just not how it works. If I even exist, other than between your ears, I'm playing the same game on the same field as all of you and the rest of the universe. I have a few tricks but under the covers there's just some random stuff way down there.

So, to summarise: when things get 'big' (I'm talking atomic sized and up) they get pretty predictable, but way down there it's more messy. Your brains, with their ridiculous 86 billion cells and the 100 trillion connections between them have their roots firmly down in that smeary soup. Sometimes you can be pretty confident about what's coming next, but not always! And that's what real free will is. Actually, almost nothing that humans do requires and entails free will, but in those occasional moments when you 'stop and think', really think, then it's there, available, and occasionally you use it (and, not to dent your hubristic naivety, so do some other 'lesser' creatures on your blue dot).

Now, even knowing all of this, what you decide to do with Pete and those other unfortunates like him is down to your 'club rules'. I notice that in your club you tend to put 'defective' humans in little boxes, out of the way. Better than some of the more whacky clubs, but given what I've just explained is really going on, you might want to consider other options. I've got some sympathy, those remarkable brains of yours are quite the business. I often wonder how something so complicated ever works properly, or at least to any acceptable level of reliability. Just a suggestion, but you might want to focus further upstream on some of your problems.

Later!

******

BETTER JUDGEMENT

ELECTION 2024

The Count

Jean Scott and her producer were mystified and nervous. This made no sense. Were people lying? Why would they? They had never done so in previous elections. But the alternative was so radical that Scott's anxiety levels were rising precipitously, hours before she was due to broadcast. Could all of the predictions be as wrong as their local statistics suggested?. Earlier in the day she had left her producer and researcher at the polling station, found a quiet spot and phoned a BBC colleague working in South London. Despite reassurance from her colleague and others that they were not an outlier she knew she might be the first reporter to declare this statistical rumour as fact and did not want to look foolish. She glanced at her watch again and looked over to the cameraman. The count was almost in, he held up an outstretched palm; five minutes to broadcast.

For years, Sunderland and Newcastle have been the first constituencies to declare their results in UK General Elections. The cities' rivalries are wide, deep and long-standing and the race to be the first to declare is as keen as any. Scott was reporting for the BBC from Houghton & Sunderland South where people were literally running around the tennis club where the count was taking place carrying boxes of ballot papers to and from tables where rows of

ELECTION 2024

tellers were confirming the final tally.

Scott's producer counted the cameraman down to the live feed to the BBC studio where Clive Myrie had just announced that Sunderland were the first to declare for 2024. They were live. Scott stood, out of shot, watching the room settle as the Returning Officer stepped onto the small stage, the six candidates shuffled into a line up behind him. He began his formulaic and characteristically stilted delivery of the result. Returning Officers read out the number of votes for each candidate in turn and then declare the winner as 'duly elected' for their constituency. They should also include in this count the number of rejected, or spoiled, ballot papers but many do not. In 2019 around 60% of all the people living in this constituency had voted; 16,210 of them for Bridget Phillipson the winning Labour candidate. Five years ago she had beaten the Conservative candidate by 3,115 votes with the Brexit candidate some way behind. Now what? The political climate had changed and Labour were in the ascendancy; everyone was expecting a large Labour majority.

An unconvincing, nervous cheer greeted Phillipson's vote count of 8,353. This was almost half what she had polled in 2019 and with only the Reform candidate left to declare, the room settled into a shocked silence knowing that based on what everyone had just heard Reform must have captured a huge slice of the vote. As the returning officer announced the final candidate's votes as 3,025 there was a moment's silence and then a shocked cheer from the Labour supporters which was subsumed by a flood of consternation from everyone in the hall. Something was dreadfully wrong.

ELECTION 2024

Before announcing the winner the Returning Officer then added, "The number of rejected ballot papers was 24,309."

Someone at the back of the room shrieked with delight and everyone turned to look at the three young people, until then unnoticed, hugging one another. Confused muttering filled the room and the Returning Officer had to shout, "I therefore declare that Bridget Phillipson has been duly elected as member for the said constituency."

For the BBC, Clive Myrie's voice interceded as, on the small stage several candidates shook Phillipson's hand but everyone appeared to be in a state of shock.

"So a Labour hold, as predicted, with the Conservatives in third place behind Reform." Myrie said, "But let's go to our reporter Jean Scott to try to understand what has just happened." Myrie glanced at the sheet of paper he was handed and then looked up, "Jean, over 60% of ballots spoiled; this is completely unprecedented, what's going on?"

Scott, in close-up, with the microphone held tight, was nodding, people milling behind her, an excited babble filling the room

"Clive, as we've been reporting all day, the exit polls suggested a significant number of people had decided not to vote for any party and to protest by spoiling their ballot. We've heard from colleagues across the country that this is happening everywhere, but we had no idea of the scale, until now. Apparently a majority of voters in Sunderland do not want any of the candidates who were on the ballot and many have written the letters WWBD on their ballots."

Scott held up a spoiled ballot paper to camera as an

example with the letters clearly visible.

"Viewers may be aware of the social media campaign which has been growing over the last weeks with the core demand 'We Want Better Democracy', so the acronym WWBD. Labour have obviously retained this seat, but in this context we have to ask, is this a legitimate mandate to form a Government? Legally, electorally, it is but if this pattern is repeated in other places around the country where does that leave a prospective Government?"

Clive Myrie's familiar voice intoned, "Where indeed, Jean." The feed cut back to the studio where Myrie and Laura Kuenssberg were at the Election 2024 desk. Myrie continued to camera, "Jean Scott there in Sunderland where the electorate seem to have delivered a message to politicians that they are far from content with the status quo. Laura, what do you make of that extraordinary and unprecedented result?"

***

On the morning after election day 2024 the United Kingdom woke to find that while most had been sleeping a quiet revolution had taken place. A few pundits who had followed the WWBD social media campaign had been predicting this possibility, but nobody had been listening. The campaign had only been running for a couple of months but had attracted attention from some important influencers from the outset. Whoever was behind it had spent a great deal of money as election day approached. The message was that party politics and the adversarial zero-sum game it increasingly represented was at the core of the countries problems and needed to change.

ELECTION 2024

All the politicians had ignored the WWBD campaign as a complete distraction. They had continued sniping and bickering, oblivious to the growing contempt with which a large percentage of the electorate viewed their behaviour. A few commentators had not been so dismissive of the unusual campaign and had looked beneath the covers. The renowned Times journalist, Matthew Seddon, had been one of them and, in his last two Sunday columns before the election, had explained how well funded and organised the campaign was, how it was on practically everybody's social media feed and was growing daily. Nobody was listening then, but they certainly were now. Seddon was being interviewed on Breakfast TV.

"Yes, I did think something along these lines could happen, and as you know, I've been writing about it for several weeks. Having said that, the scale of it is well beyond what I anticipated. I thought it might be a protest of maybe five or at most ten percent of voters. People have been disaffected with politics for a long time but until now there seemed to be no alternative. But a majority of the electorate, no, I did not believe it would be anything like this and neither did anyone else. Early analysis suggests that in some constituencies seventy five percent of voters under thirty five voted for WWBD, if voting is the right term. As to who is behind this campaign, we still don't know. There are rumours that it is a group of philanthropic donors from the United States, and many believe George Soros who has donated billions to pro-democracy causes in recent years may be involved, but as I say these are still just rumours."

ELECTION 2024

People did not have to wait for long to discover who was behind the campaign; the WWBD website added a new 'About Us' page. As a measure of how robust their technology and planning was, the millions of hits the site received in the first hour would normally have been deemed a denial of service attack, but the site did not crash. A man, completely unknown, by the name of Paul Croft, was found to be the head of, or at least the spokesman for, WWBD. They had an office in a non-descript co-working building close to London Bridge Station which they had occupied for only 6 months. By eleven o'clock several hundred reporters and camera crews were vying for space at the office entrance. Anyone who worked in the building had to thread an intimidating corridor of lenses and microphones, being asked if they worked for WWBD. So far none of them did.

WWBD announced that at midday Paul Croft would address the press to explain what their movement, as they were now calling it, was trying to achieve. As with everything this new movement was doing, the timing of their press conference was no accident; it coincided with the Labour leader's meeting with the King at Buckingham Palace to, presumably, be asked to form the new government. Presumably, because it was abundantly clear that despite having 'won' the election the electorate had effectively voted for none of the traditional parties. They had voted for change and as people explored the WWBD website they were discovering what form this change might take.

Manifesto For Change

Paul Croft walked out to the front entrance of the office to find the road blocked with journalists and camera crews. The police had closed the station approach to prevent cars entering the street and were redirecting traffic. He was accompanied by two women, one carrying a plastic bottle crate. She placed it on the ground just outside the office doors and after a brief word between Croft and the two women he stood on the box to an explosion of noise and flashing camera lights. He had no notes and stood for a moment surveying the crowd with a trace of a smile on his face. Whether he was nervous was hard to tell, he appeared calm, one hand cupped around a wrist, his arms held loosely in front. He was about 40 years old, tall, mid brown hair, wearing a casual pair of trousers and a light grey T-shirt. He was completely unremarkable. He stood and waited as the shouted questions began to subside and everyone realised he would not speak until there was silence. When all that could be heard was the traffic a few hundred meters away in Borough High Street he began.

"It has been clear to many for some time that the democratic systems in our country have not been serving us well. It makes little difference which party is in power, the constraints on them are the same and the problems they face, the same. To expect a few people at the head of these parties to have all the answers we need in our complex and increasingly polarised world is naïve. A politician's primary job is to be elected. To do this they tell the electorate, us, what they think we want to hear and every few years we have the unedifying spectacle which we have just witnessed. If this is the best a country like Great Britain can do, then we should be concerned for all our futures."

He paused and allowed the muttering to ebb and silence to return. He might be unknown but he had been taught how to deal with a crowd.

"We believe there are better ways to organise a democracy …"

"Who's 'we'?" called a voice from the crowd and others shouted their endorsement of the question."

Croft nodded, "We are funded by a group of philanthropic organisations and individuals who believe that a new version of democracy would serve the world well. We chose to begin here in the United Kingdom, but we believe our new model will benefit societies across the globe. Shortly, our website will list all of the supporters who wish to be identified." He paused and with a hint of a smile added, "Which is all of them, because a condition of their support was that they had to be willing to be identified."

"Including how much they have donated?" a voice called.

"Yes." Croft replied, simply.

"Well Labour have just won the election with a huge majority, so it's not working very well so far, is it Mr Croft?" Another voice called.

Croft raised his eyebrows, "Well we will see. As one of the BBC reporters said, Labour have won but, in the circumstances, does this give them the moral right to form a government. The answer to that is clearly no, a majority of those who chose to vote want something other than one of the traditional parties. Will something as inconvenient as a majority actively voting for something else prevent Labour attempting to form a government? I doubt it, but we will see."

"Do you want to be Prime Minster, Mr Croft?"

Croft smiled at this. "Nobody voted for me, I cannot command the confidence of the house of commons, as is the requirement for that office. No."

"So what do you want Mr Croft?"

"We would like to propose a different way of organising our democracy. A system which a majority of people in this country will support. It is a way of making decisions free from the short term constraints of the electoral cycle and will allow us to plan for our long-term futures."

"So you want to get rid of elections, something more like the Chinese Communist Party, perhaps." A voice shouted, followed by some laughter.

"How did you guess, yes that's exactly right." Croft said and in the uproar that followed he raised his hands, clearly enjoying himself. And when he could be heard said, "No nothing remotely like that."

The surprise that he would wind up the reporters in this way caused a wash of amazed chatter and some amusement and Croft had to wait again for quiet to descend.

"We simply believe the citizens of our country should have a larger say in the way it is run. But we do need to alter the way everything is tied to party politics and the election cycle."

"You're stuck with the electoral cycle if you still have elections, mate." Someone shouted.

Croft nodded. "Or maybe not. One idea, and this is only one of many, not what we are necessarily promoting, would be to re-elect 1/5th of our MPs every year, so that they all change on a five year cycle and each one stands for five years before seeking re-election, as they do now."

There was muttering and conversations broke out across the throng and Croft waited yet again for their attention to refocus on him, "As I said, that is one idea and we have others. However at the centre of everything would be ordinary citizens making informed decisions about policy."

"Citizen's assemblies." was shouted.

"Exactly. If they are conducted well they provide well considered, robust, democratic decisions. So with that I'm going to ask you all to go away and bone up on citizen's assemblies and we'll get together again soon to talk in more detail about how we can create a stronger democracy and work for a more equitable and secure future for Great Britain. Thankyou." He jumped down, one of the women grabbed the crate and in seconds all three were through the glass doors and walking away without looking back at the stunned mass of press, vainly shouting questions after them.".

Parliament

The state opening of parliament was on 9th of July just five days after the General Election. Labour had a majority of 180 seats and had elected to form the Government amid increasingly loud protests from various groups. The opposition parties were in a cleft stick; unhappy about the scale of Labour's majority but lacking any democratic mandate of their own. The only constant was the usual internal party factions arguing amongst themselves. Groups in civil society, emboldened, were arguing for a re-run of the election with a different voting system. Each nuanced flavour of proportional representation was being touted as the answer by its advocates. Meanwhile the new WWBD movement was setting out their vision for the future and amassing millions of followers.

Paul Croft had, briefly, become a global celebrity but the movement made it clear that he was simply a spokesperson for an organisation that made decisions as a group. The two women who had accompanied Croft, Sania Hussein the CEO of an IT company which Croft had once worked for and Grace Sommers, until recently a Metropolitan Police detective, were splashed across social media, both, briefly hounded after the press conference. Attention was slowly dying, other than in the tabloids and more lurid sections of social media. Both women, being attractive, has spawned deepfakes in porn videos available to anyone who cared to search. For almost 48 hours the WWBD movement ignored all of this, offering 'no comment' to every enquiry. They made no demands, and on their web site set out a model for government where political parties effectively had no power. Instead citizens' assemblies were used to set policy and the way the cabinet worked would be transformed. Ministers could no longer be shuffled in and out at the whim of the Prime Minister. Once selected they were in the job for their elected tenure unless forced out by bad behaviour or incompetence. They would be made responsible for their department's performance. There were a myriad other proposed changes aimed at stopping short-term incentives and thinking with proposals to ensure that domain knowledge and deep expertise in the Civil Service would be rewarded over time.

Almost everyone thought the proposals would deliver better government, except, inevitably, the new Government. The media attempted to fulfil its now traditional role of ringmaster, tempting Paul Croft to commit to various political outcomes, but to no avail. He reverted each time to the fact that WWBD espoused a process not policy solutions. The new organisation was well organised, very well funded and supported by the smartest constitution lawyers and democratic experts available and they were in the ascendancy.

***

Unbeknownst to most people, a year before the election someone from the nascent movement had persuaded Doreen Dixon, the then Secretary of State for Digital, Culture, Media and Sport to hold a citizens assembly which considered changes to the UK's misuse of drugs act. The assembly had proposed radical measures to decriminalise most narcotics with a roadmap over several years to legalise many and to license them as we now do alcohol and tobacco. It was a clever strategy, understanding the public's mood and that of most of the country's law enforcement agencies. All understood that 'The War On Drugs' could never be won and had, in reality, been lost years ago. A heavy majority of the public knew this and wanted change but government's fear of the media was so strong that neither Conservative or Labour, would touch the recommendations with the proverbial barge poll, however democratically legitimate or logically sound.

In the assembly the proposals had been created and voted

for by 68% of the participants, about 2 to 1; a consensus typical of these types of assemblies. The new proposals would save the country billions of pounds a year, people would be treated rather than imprisoned and based on experience in other parts of the world, overall drug use would broadly stay the same. It sounded radical, but other countries had already been guinea pigs for similar policy changes. For the new Labour government it was fabulously tempting. Initiated by a Conservative government, democratically safe, it promised huge savings for the economy and to prevent the needless death of thousands each year. If it failed it would be the Conservative's fault, if it succeeded it would be a result of Labour's strong democratic instincts and foresight. Some in the government warned that this was an obvious Trojan horse; but it was irresistible.

Social media was awash with opinion and memes overwhelmingly supportive of the new citizen centred democracy. The idea that the politicians were no longer 'in charge' was what many voices had long been calling for. Now it had a physical form and there was a growing call for WWBD to replace the new Labour Government. That idea might have been a constitutional nightmare, except that the United Kingdom does not have a written constitution.

One Year Later

Paul Croft, Grace Sommers and Gail Bailey-Royce, a well known human rights lawyer and an adviser to the WWBD movement from its inception, arrived at Downing Street for the weekly Cabinet meeting. None were members of the

Government but the popular clamour for their inclusion at the heart of Government from the media and the public had long ago become too loud to resist.

Recent elections in France and Germany had been massively influenced by the result of the UK election and in Germany 173 members of the Bundestag had been elected, having been randomly selected as representatives of the German WWBD, 'Wir wollen eine bessere Demokratie'. They held the balance of power in parliament and all were independent of any political party.

In the UK three very public citizen's assemblies were in progress to consider changes to specific parts of the NHS, immigration and housing, respectively. Four other assemblies were in planning. The Labour Government was enjoying record approval ratings and in public trumpeting its democratic credentials. In private almost every party politician was wondering where this would lead. Many felt like turkeys cheering for an approaching festive season.

Cabinet was discussing a radical WWBD proposal to abolish the Whips system; or at least to radically change their remit. Whips are the way UK parties control their members in government. They are a group of administrators appointed to control each party's members and every junior MP knows that when the whips call, you answer; no ifs, no buts and if you don't toe the party line you will never achieve high office. Older MPs who have accepted their lot can defy the whips and MPs in small parties, not subject to whip control, are allowed, up to a point, to vote as they see fit on any particular issue. When MPs in the main parties are told, via a three line whip, to vote for a piece of legislation they overwhelmingly do. There is no need to read the details of the proposals or to think deeply about its effects on people. It is Government policy and they do as they are told. For MPs, the idea that they might express an opinion about legislation without suffering some form of sanction was seductive. The party leaders were dead set against this change, arguing that the whips were essential in order that manifesto policies could pass unhindered through Parliament. In the face of the electorate's effective 'vote' for WWBD this claim was hard to stand up.

Gail Bailey-Royce was, once again, reiterating the WWBD's position, "They are one of the most criticised parts of our democratic system. We understand why you want to keep them, it's how you control your MPs, but along with many other things their time has come. If we want to improve the quality of our legislation and to serve the people of this country better, this has to change."

The Prime Minister glanced across the Cabinet table at Bailey-Royce, irritated at her calm assurance and perpetual air of intimidating competence and then looked off into space again. He was running out of road, obfuscating and delaying for as long as he could. WWBD were completely dominating the conversation on social media and one of his cabinet ministers had almost been laughed off the stage in a recent BBC debate in which Paul Croft had been cheered by most of the audience. They were a Government in name only and they would soon be faced with a choice.

"This would destroy the workings of Government, we've

been over this." Starmer said, without conviction.

"That does not appear to reflect the thinking of your MPs. Do I really have to show you the informal numbers we have on this?" Bailey-Royce replied, calmly.

"No, you don't." There was clear irritation in the Prime Minsters voice. "I'm beginning to feel like a puppet with the hand of WWBD stuck up my back and regardless of the minority of the electorate who voted for us, ours is the party they voted for. You would do well to remember that. You are all here with our forbearance."

A number of ministers looked down and shuffled back slightly in their seats. They had never seen the Prime Minister react like this and they knew exactly how Bailey-Royce would react.

She was completely unperturbed and her demeanour did not change, "Prime Minister, If you could remove us from here, you would have done so already; I think we all know that. Our collective job is to serve the British People as best we can and you have seen all the polling and focus group data. The project we are all engaged in is overwhelmingly what the citizens of this country want. Your Government's approval ratings are through the roof, you are in danger of going down as the most popular Prime Minister since the second world war. I do not understand why you are fighting this. It almost exactly aligns with your core beliefs and that of your party."

It was hard for her not to sound like she was talking to a petulant child and everyone in the room could see that she was trying not to undermine the Prime Minister. People were shuffling uncomfortably.

She continued, "Prime Minister, you can transform democracy in this country and benefit millions of lives and lead the way for the rest of the world as this country used to do. We can see this already happening in some other countries, it's the start of a new wave of democracy and you can have your name indelibly stamped on this."

She was good, there was no doubt about it, and a many of the ministers were now unconsciously and some consciously agreeing with her, leaning in, nodding.

"That old model is fading, it's the past and you can lead Great Britain into the future."

As the doors of their car closed, Paul Croft turned to the back seat. "Absolute masterclass, Gail."

Grace Sommers had her hand on Gail's on the seat and she was smiling out of the window.

Gail gave a half smile, "If he's not too stubborn he'll go down in history as one of our greatest Prime Ministers and if he won't budge he'll get buried. All I did was march him to the edge of the cliff and make him look out."

Another Year Later

Revolutions come in may forms and this was a quiet one, but a revolution it certainly was. Two years, almost to the day after the general election, Parliament voted on a bill that meant it was the last of its kind; at least until the next revolution. One in five MPs would face re-election in the coming year, at a date to be agreed, in what was being called an Annual

Election. The constituencies for each of the first annual elections were to be randomly selected so that a different 130 seats would be elected each time. When this first cycle was complete some MPs would have served more than seven years, but thereafter each would serve five.

The political parties would remain, but their power would henceforth rest in their ability to persuade both citizens and elected MPs with the strength of their arguments. The political scientists who had devised this system believed that allegiance to political parties would fade over time and constituencies would form, instead, around single ideas and causes. Policy would be determined by citizens' assemblies; those advocating for change would present their ideas to these assemblies and citizens would decide.

None of these changes would instantly make the economy grow or would staff the NHS at levels people would like, or pay teachers more, but all of these things would be addressed and decided upon by the people for the people. It would be hard for a Union to ask its members to strike in the face of a majority of citizens agreeing upon the terms of a settlement. Big business was facing a serious crisis in terms of how it lobbied government. Having the ear of a minister and quietly offering a well paid directorship for little effort when they left power was pointless. Ministers no longer decided policy, they were simply responsible for implementing it.

The quality of legislation would begin to improve and every department had to report publicly on the progress they were making. Ministers would become more like CEOs and would be judged by the way their departments performed, not whether they would support the Prime Minister in a confidence vote.

***

Kier Starmer would go on to be regarded as one of the country's great reformers, starting a wave of what became global citizen democracy. History sometimes misses some of the important detail, but that was just fine for all of those quiet revolutionaries at WWBD who got what they wanted, Better Democracy.

******

ABOUT THE AUTHOR

Peter is an engineer, at least temperamentally if not professionally. He made stuff up (software) for a few decades and is now making other stuff up (stories and novels). Engineers like to know how things work and cannot avoid being offended when they work badly. It's hard to make things better in our increasingly complex world and there is plenty that could do with an upgrade, but people don't want to be told how to change. Perhaps the best way is to tell them a story; try to infect them with that most virulent of things, a new idea.

Peter and his wife preside over an empty nest in South London, their 2 adult children fledged into an increasingly difficult world. He has not abandoned the idea that with some persistence and smart thinking he could make the world a little less difficult for them and many others.

Printed in Great Britain
by Amazon